Paddington
Goes to Hospital

MICHAEL BOND & KAREN JANKEL

ILLUSTRATED BY R.W. ALLEY

Collins

Paddington lay back on the lawn with his paws in the air and gazed up at the Browns. "Where am I?" he gasped.

"You're at home, dear," said Mrs Brown. "At number thirty-two, Windsor Gardens."

"Is that in Darkest Peru?" asked Paddington.

"If you ask me," said Mrs Bird, "that bear's lost his memory."

"Oh dear, Henry!" exclaimed Mrs Brown. "What shall we do?"

Mr Brown consulted his Medical Dictionary. "All it says here is, 'the victim shouldn't drive a car'."

"I don't think I could anyway," said Paddington.

"I've hurt my shoulder."

"Would you like a bun?" suggested Mrs Brown.

"What's a bun?" asked Paddington.

"That settles it," said Mrs Bird.

"I'm phoning the hospital!"

"I'm sorry we took so long," said the ambulance driver.
"When I heard the name 'Paddington' I went to the railway
station by mistake. If you ask me," he added, "this young
bear's not only lost his memory, he's put his shoulder out as
well. One of you ladies had better come with him in case he
has to stay in hospital overnight."

"Thank goodness I put his clean pyjamas out this
morning," said Mrs Bird, trying to strike a cheerful note.

The ambulance crew soon made up for lost time, and with sirens wailing, Paddington reached the hospital in no time at all.

"Stand by for a young bear emergency," said the driver to the waiting staff, and with a count of three, they lifted Paddington on to a bed.

"Is it true that you've lost your memory?" asked a doctor.

"Would you mind repeating the question?" replied Paddington. "Phew! Phew!"

"I don't like the sound of his wheezes," said a nurse.

"I think we've got complications," agreed the doctor. "He'd better go straight to x-ray."

"You've got complications!" exclaimed Paddington indignantly. "What about me? Phew! Phew!"

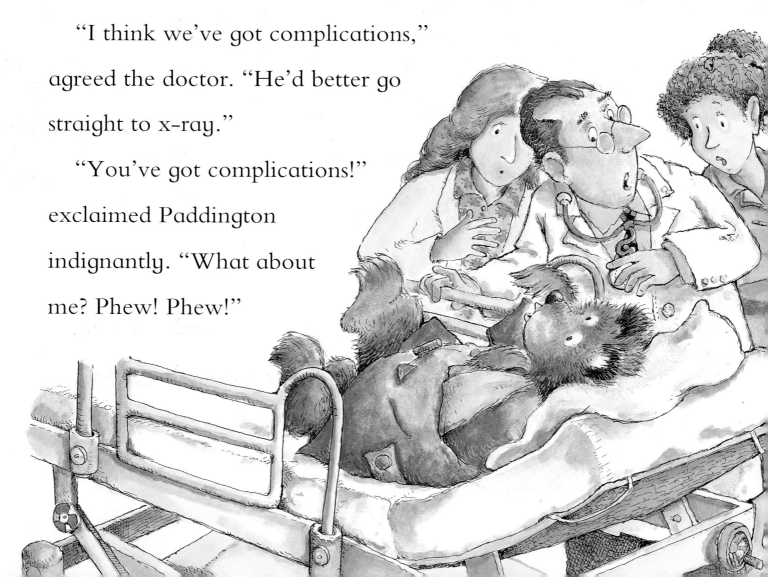

Paddington had never travelled anywhere on a bed before and he thought it was very good value. "There was nothing like this in Darkest Peru," he announced as they gathered speed. "Phew! Phew!"

When they reached the x-ray room, the lady in charge pushed a large machine over the bed and made some adjustments.

"Now lie very still while I take some pictures," she said. "Otherwise, they will come out blurred."

With that she went to the other side of the room, pressed a button, and there was a whirring noise.

"Cheese!" said Paddington.

Afterwards, Paddington and Mrs Brown met the doctor again.

Paddington stared at the pictures on the wall. "What's happened to my fur?" he exclaimed. "I had it when I came in."

"It's still there," said the doctor. "This is a special camera for looking inside people – and bears, too," he added hastily.

"It looks very complicated," said Paddington. "I didn't know I had so much inside me."

"The one on the left shows why your shoulder's hurting," explained the doctor. "The bone's come out of its socket. We shall need to put you to sleep while we relocate it."

"Have you had anything to eat since breakfast?" asked a nurse.

"I haven't even had time for my elevenses," said Paddington.

"That's good," said the nurse,
wiping his arm with something cold.
"Otherwise you would have had to
wait while it settled."

Paddington felt a tiny prick,
and he was about to give the
nurse a hard stare...

...when his eyelids began to go droopy.

As soon as he was asleep the doctor turned to Mrs Brown. "We'll soon put things right. He won't feel a thing.

"As for his memory, it probably needs a jog, but a good night's rest often works wonders. I must say I'm a bit worried about his breathing, though."

"It's a mystery," said Mrs Brown. "He's never had this problem before."

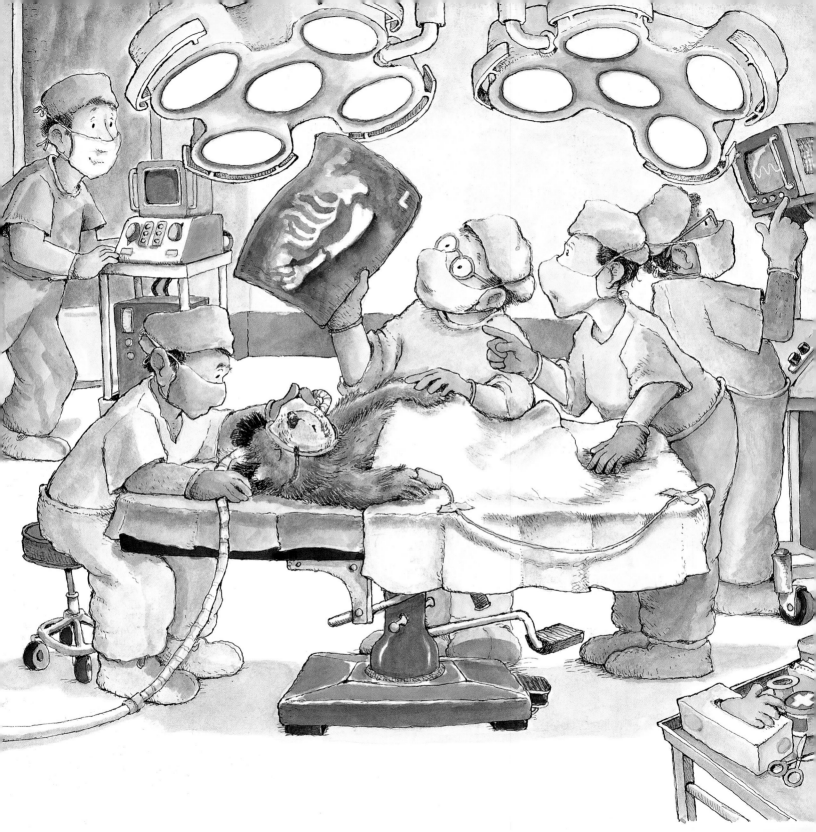

Paddington woke to find himself in a strange room.

"Where am I?" he asked for the second time that day.

"You're in a ward with lots of other patients," said Mrs Brown. "And the doctor's put your arm back in its socket."

"I hope it's pointing the right way," said Paddington. "Otherwise, I shan't know whether I'm coming or going."

"I've brought you some water," said a nurse. "I expect you're feeling thirsty after your operation."

"I am," said Paddington.

He was about to ask for something more exciting to drink, but he couldn't think of the name.

"Tea?" suggested Mrs Brown.

"Bless you!" said Paddington.

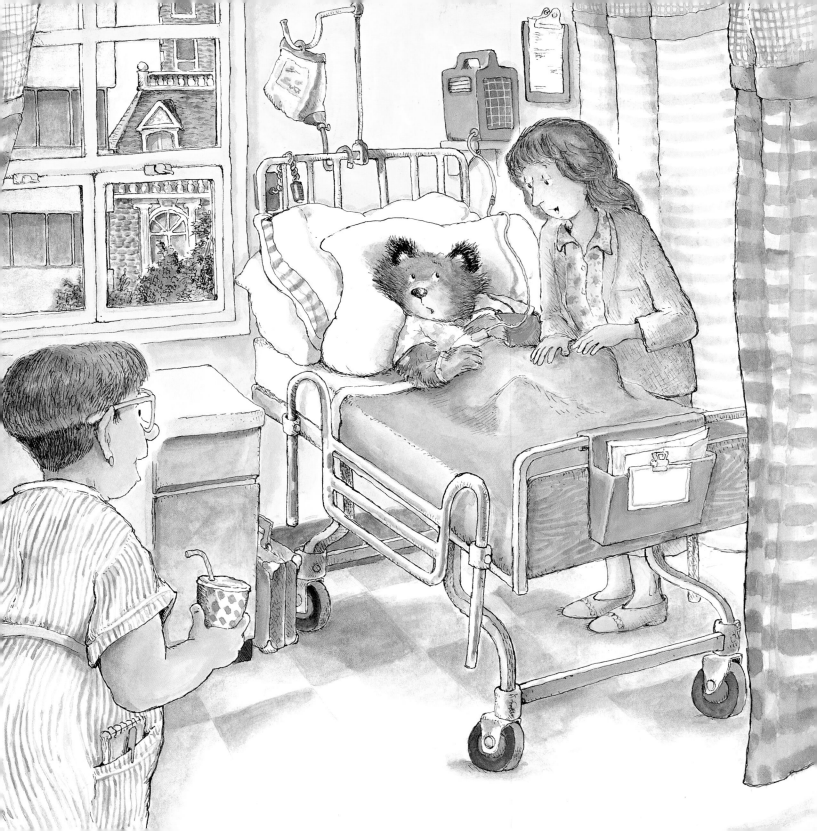

"I expect they will keep you in overnight for observation," said Mrs Brown.

"I don't think I want anyone observing me asleep," said Paddington. "I might fall out of bed."

"Don't worry," said the nurse. "The sides lift up to stop that happening."

"Besides, I shan't be far away," said Mrs Brown.

At that moment Mr Brown arrived, carrying a bowl of fruit from all the traders in the market and a 'Get Well Soon' card from Paddington's friend, Mr Gruber.

"Even Mr Curry sent his best wishes," he said. "What it is to be popular."

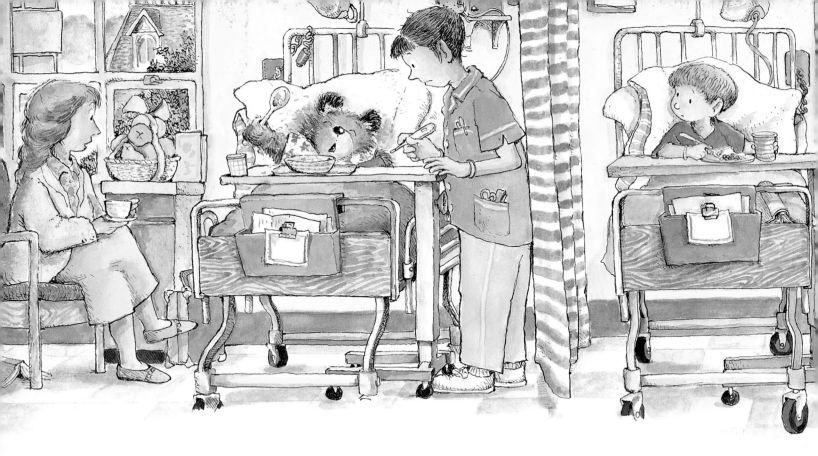

The lady who brought Paddington's supper had been surprised to see him. "The boy who used to be in your bed liked his food hot and spicy," she warned. "I hope it's suitable for bears."

Paddington had told her not to worry.

"There's nothing wrong with your appetite," said a nurse, eyeing the empty plate.

"There is now!" gasped Paddington. And this time his "phews!" sounded as though he really meant them, for he had never before tasted anything quite so hot.

"I think I'd better leave taking your temperature until you've cooled down," said the nurse. "I'll simply feel your pulse to be going on with."

Just then two more nurses came along, pushing a trolley laden with bottles and jars.

"It's medicine time," said one of them, handing Paddington a small cup filled with pink liquid.

"I'd like another one of those, please," he announced.

"I think it's doing me good already."

The nurse laughed. "I wish we had more patients like you."

"It's all your fault, Henry," said Mrs Brown. "No wonder Paddington lost his memory."

"Well, at least it seems to have been jogged back again," said Mr Brown defensively.

"Phew! Phew!" agreed Paddington.

"And that's another thing," said Mrs Bird. She held up a small silver object. "Guess what?"

"It's the present you gave me in case I ever have an emergency," said Paddington. "It must have fallen out of my pocket." He held the object up to his mouth and blew, "Phew! Phew!"

Several piercing blasts brought doctors and nurses running from all directions.

"It's nice to know it isn't broken. When I lost my memory, I forgot I needed a whistle to make my 'phews' work," said Paddington.

"All's well that ends well," said the doctor, as the Browns explained what had happened.

"It's been a learning experience for us, too," he added, amid general agreement.

"It could come in very useful if we have any more bear patients to look after."

"I'm glad you had me to practise on," said Paddington, as he waved goodbye.

"I've never been in a hospital before, and now that I know what goes on, I shall never mind coming back!"